CONTENTS

PUBLISHED BY PETER HADDOCK LTD
BRIDLINGTON ENGLAND
© PETER HADDOCK LTD
Printed in Russia
ISBN 0-7105-0466-7

Sleeping Beauty

Retold and Illustrated by John Patience

There was once a King and Queen who dearly
wanted a child and after many years the Queen gave
birth to a baby daughter. To show his pleasure the
King gave a magnificent christening feast and
ordered his scribes to invite the six good fairies of
the Kingdom as guests of honour. It was a wonderful
occasion. There was plenty of good food, music from

the King's minstrels, a troup of acrobats and a juggler. When the feast was over the fairies stepped up one by one to bestow their blessings on the baby. She would have the temper of an angel, sing as sweetly as a nightingale, dance like a leaf on the breeze, be as beautiful as a summer's day, as graceful as a swan and . . .

Suddenly the door was flung open and in strode a seventh fairy. She was very old and extremely angry at having been forgotten. She greeted no-one, but screamed out a horrible curse that the Princess would one day prick her finger on a spindle and die. A terrible silence fell upon the room, but the youngest fairy, who had not yet bestowed her blessing, spoke up, saying, "I cannot undo the curse, but I can soften it. The Princess will indeed pierce her finger on a spindle, though she will not die, but fall into a deep sleep that will last for a hundred years."

The King was filled with fear. He gave orders that
every spindle in the land should be destroyed in a
bonfire, lest the fairy's curse should be fulfilled. The
years passed and the Princess grew up to be all that
the good fairies had promised. Then one day at the
age of fifteen, she was wandering about the castle
when she came upon a room at the top of a tower. In
a keyhole in the door was a glittering, golden key.
The Princess reached out and turned it and the door
swung open. In front of her sat an old woman,
quietly spinning at her wheel. The Princess had
never seen a spinning wheel before and was eager to
try it, but no sooner had she taken up the wool from
the spindle than she pricked her finger and fell into a
deep sleep. At this the old lady, who was really the
wicked fairy, let out a horrible peal of laughter and
disappeared.

The wicked fairy's laughter echoed all around the castle and brought the King's soldiers rushing into the room, but it was obvious that nothing could be done to help the Princess. With tears in his eyes, the King carried his daughter to her bed and laid her to rest. Then he, too, began to fall under the wicked fairy's spell, as did everyone else in the castle. One by one the courtiers, the cooks, the guards and the footmen, the pigeons on the rooftops, the horses in the stables, cats, dogs and mice – all fell into a profound slumber. The years passed by and a great tangle of thorns grew up around the castle and together with the thorns grew the legend of the Sleeping Beauty.

Many brave young men came to try to rescue the beautiful Princess, but they were all caught in the vicious thicket of thorns and died horrible deaths!

Now a hundred years had passed and a Prince from another land came riding by. He saw the ragged flags fluttering from the turrets which peeped above the thicket and asked an old man about the castle. The old man, who had heard the story of the Sleeping Beauty from his grandfather, told it to the Prince, but he left him with a warning. "If you value your life" he said, "you will forget the Sleeping Beauty and return home." The Prince, however, was valiant and decided to hack his way through the thorns. Amazingly, no sooner had he drawn his sword than the thicket parted and a safe pathway opened up before him.

As the Prince entered the enchanted castle the sound of his footsteps echoed down the corridors and through the dusty halls, breaking the silence of a century. Everywhere he went he came upon people wrapped in deepest sleep and draped in veils of cobwebs. He wandered on through the labyrinth of the castle with his heartbeat pounding in his ears, but he became more and more afraid and wished himself out in the warm sunshine, far away from this eerie, deathly place.

17

At last he came to a staircase which led to the door of a small bedchamber. He entered and there he found the sleeping Princess. In wonder the Prince stooped over the bed and gently kissed her on the lips. The Princess's eyelids fluttered and opened and as she looked upon the Prince they fell in love. And so the hundred years curse was broken.

19

At the moment the Princess awoke from her sleep, so did everyone else and soon the castle was full of life and merry-making. The King and Queen were over-joyed to see their daughter again and everyone said what a wonderful couple she and the Prince made.

Not long after that, the two of them married and, waving goodbye, set out on a journey to the Prince's land, where they lived together in peace and happiness to the end of their days.

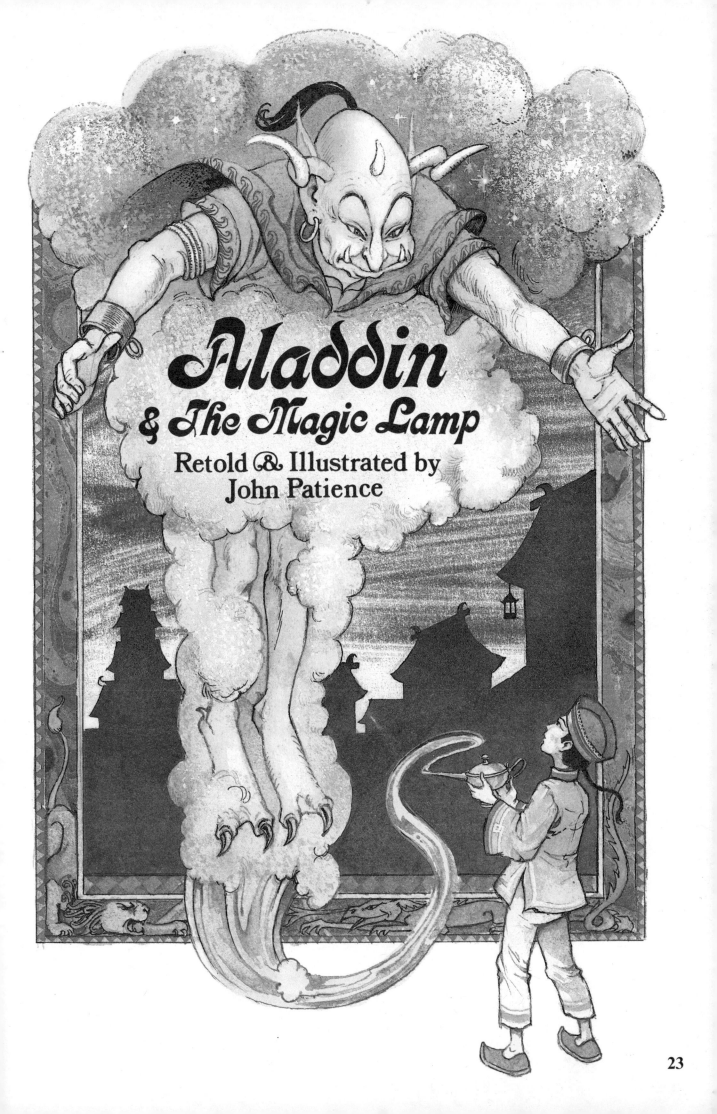

Aladdin
& The Magic Lamp

Retold & Illustrated by
John Patience

This is the story of a young man named Aladdin who lived with his widowed mother in a city in China, long, long ago. One day Aladdin was talking with his friends in the street when a stranger approached him. He was an evil magician called Abenazer who had travelled all the way from Africa to carry out a secret plan. "My boy," said Abenazer, "I can make you extremely rich if you will only help me with a small task." Now Aladdin and his mother were very poor and so he was eager and willing to help.

Abenazer took Aladdin to a place where a narrow tunnel led down into the mountainside. "At the end of the tunnel you will find a magic garden where precious jewels grow on trees," said the magician. "You may help yourself to them. All I want is the ancient bronze lamp that burns in the garden. There are dangers in the tunnel, but wear this ring and it will protect you."

Aladdin made his way down the tunnel to the magic garden where, as Abenazer had promised, he found the ancient lamp and the beautiful jewelled

trees. Snuffing out the lamp he put it into his
pocket. He picked some of the jewels and then
crept back up to the mouth of the tunnel. "I see
you have the lamp!" cried Abenazer. "Give it to
me at once!" Aladdin refused to do this until he
was out of the tunnel. At this, Abenazer became
extremely angry and, screaming out some magic
words, he sealed up the tunnel's entrance, leaving
Aladdin imprisoned underground.

For two days the boy remained, crying in the
dark. Then he accidentally rubbed the ring which
Abanezer had given him. Immediately an enormous
genie appeared, saying, "I am the slave of the ring
and am ready to obey you. What is your wish?"
"Please take me out of this place," cried the
startled Aladdin. In a moment he found himself
standing outside the tunnel in the open air.

When Aladdin arrived back home, his mother was overjoyed to see him. He told her the story of his adventures and showed her the old brass lamp. "How strange," she said. "Why should Abenazer want this old lamp so badly? Look how dirty it is." And she rubbed it with her sleeve to shine it up. Suddenly there was a deafening BANG and a huge genie came pouring like smoke from the lamp, saying, "Behold, I am the genie of the lamp – the greatest of all the genies. What is your wish?" Aladdin's mother was terrified, but Aladdin, who had seen a genie before, replied, "I am hungry. Please fetch me something to eat." In a moment the kitchen table was spread with a marvellous feast. Aladdin quickly realised the incredible power of the lamp and why Abenazer had wanted it so much. He commanded the genie to bring fine clothes for his mother and himself and to transform their humble house into a grand palace, and in an instant it was done.

One day Aladdin happened to see the Emperor's daughter, the beautiful princess Badoobadoor riding by on her elephant, and he immediately fell in love with her. He decided there and then that he would marry her. Summoning the genie of the lamp, Aladdin gave his orders and the genie provided him with a dozen slaves, each with a basin filled with gold and jewels. Aladdin then went to visit the Emperor. Offering him the jewels, Aladdin proclaimed his love for princess Badoobadoor and begged for her hand in marriage. The Emperor was very impressed with Aladdin and his splendid gifts. As for Badoobadoor, she had fallen as deeply in love with Aladdin as he had with her. The Emperor gave his consent and they were married the next day.

However, the evil magician Abenazer had not forgotten Aladdin and the lamp and used his magic arts to discover that, instead of perishing in the cave, he had escaped and married the princess. Choosing a day when Aladdin was away on a hunting trip, Abenazer bought a dozen copper lamps, put them in a basket and disguised himself as a peddlar. He then went to the palace, crying, "New lamps for old. Bring me your old lamps and I will give you new ones for them!" The princess heard this strange cry and, remembering a dirty old lamp belonging to Aladdin, she sent a slave to fetch it and exchange if for a bright new one. Little did she know that she had given away Aladdin's most treasured possession.

Abenazer was filled with a wicked glee. The magic lamp was his at last! He went out of the city gates to a lonely place where he remained until nightfall, when he rubbed the lamp. The genie appeared and at Abenazer's command transported Aladdin's palace and the princess in it to a far-off place in Africa.

When Aladdin returned home he was amazed. Where was his palace, his beautiful wife and his magic lamp? Gone! What was he to do? He wrung his hands in despair and accidentally rubbed the magic ring. "What do you wish?" said the genie of the ring as he appeared. "Bring me back my palace and my dear wife," replied Aladdin. "What you ask," said the genie, "Is not within my power. Only the genie of the lamp can do that." "Then take me to the spot where my palace is," commanded

Aladdin. He had barely finished speaking before he heard the wind roaring in his ears as the genie picked him up and whisked him at incredible speed to Africa where the palace now stood. He set him down under a tree by Badoobadoor's window and disappeared. It was night and Aladdin slept soundly until next morning, when he was roused by the princess opening her window.

The princess was overjoyed to see Aladdin again and told him of how Abenazer held her prisoner and came to visit her every day. Aladdin gave her a deadly poison which he told her to pour into the magician's wine glass. Then he hid himself behind a screen. When Abenazer came to visit that day, instead of greeting him with tears and pleading for him to let her go, the princess welcomed him with a glass of poisoned wine. The magician accepted it eagerly, drained it to the last drop and fell down dead. Then Aladdin came out from his hiding place and, taking the lamp from Abenazer's pocket, he summoned the genie. "Take us home," he cried and in the winking of an eye the palace was back in China where it belonged. You may be sure that Aladdin and Badoobadoor lived there happily for the rest of their lives.

Rip van Winkle

Retold & Illustrated by John Patience

Long ago in North America, in a village at the foot of the Catskill mountains, lived a man called Rip van Winkle. Rip was a good-natured man who was always ready to lend his neighbours a helping hand, or listen to their troubles. He was very popular with everyone, but best of all Rip liked to spend his time with his little daughter and the other village children. He taught them to fly kites, carved them boats to sail and told them long stories of ghosts, witches and Indians.

Unfortunately, Rip's wife did not share other people's good opinion of her husband. She had a terrible temper and nagged poor Rip from morning till night. "You are always willing to help other people," she complained, "but you will never do a stroke of work at home. Our farm is falling into ruins and your family is dressed in rags." To escape from his wife's temper, Rip would often take his gun and go hunting in the Catskill mountains.

One day, on one of his hunting expeditions, Rip was surprised to hear someone calling his name. "Rip van Winkle! Rip van Winkle!" Rip turned and saw a strange little man toiling up the mountain side. He was bending under the weight of a barrel which he carried on his back. The stranger asked Rip to help him, and though he was a little frightened, Rip took the barrel and lifted it on to his shoulder.

The stranger showed the way and Rip went on ahead, clambering up a narrow gully. As he climbed he heard a sound like distant thunder. It made him feel rather uneasy. Presently they arrived at a level clearing. There, to Rip's astonishment, he saw a number of other strangely dressed little men. They were playing a game which looked like bowls, and it was the noise of the balls rolling which Rip had mistaken for thunder!

When the dwarves noticed Rip they stopped their game and began to stare at him. They stared so hard that Rip's knees began to knock together and his heart to pound.

The little men took the barrel from Rip and filled their flagons from it, after which they returned to their game. Eventually Rip's fear left him and, as no one was taking any notice of him, and he was feeling thirsty, he decided to try the drink himself. He filled a large bottle and took a drink from it. The flavour was excellent, but the more he drank the more thirsty he became.

After a while, the dwarves did stop their game and the one who appeared to be their commander came over to watch Rip, who, by this time, was feeling very drowsy.

At last Rip's senses were overpowered, the faces of the little men swam before his eyes, his head began to nod and he fell into a deep, deep sleep.

When Rip awoke, it was a bright and sunny morning. "Surely," he thought, "I have not slept here all night." He looked around for signs of the little men, but they were nowhere to be seen. Stranger still, Rip found that brambles had tangled themselves around him while he slept and his clothes had become tattered and torn.

Slowly Rip struggled to his feet, his back was aching and his legs were stiff. With great difficulty he began to make his way down the mountain. To his astonishment everything seemed different; the paths had become overgrown and mountain streams now bubbled and flowed where there had not even been a trickle of water before.

When he reached the village, he met a number of
people, but no one he recognised; this surprised him
because he thought he knew everyone who lived in his
village. These people were dressed in a new fashion and
they stared at Rip and whispered about him as he
passed. The dogs chased after Rip, barking at him as if
he were a stranger.

It was not easy for Rip to find his way home. The streets were all different and new buildings had sprung up everywhere. "Can it be," he thought, "that all these changes have happened overnight?" At last Rip stood in front of his own house, but he could hardly believe his eyes. It was in ruins and looked as if it had not been lived in for years!

Rip wandered away feeling very puzzled. Suddenly he caught sight of himself in a shop window. He gasped; his reflection was that of a very old man with a long white beard! No wonder people had stared, no wonder his legs were so stiff. Now he realised that he must have slept for a great deal longer than one night – more like a hundred years. Perhaps there would not be a single person left in the village who would remember him.

By this time a large crowd had gathered around Rip. "I'm Rip van Winkle," he cried. "Doesn't anyone remember me?" Most of the people thought the old man must be mad. But then a young woman came out of the crowd and took him by the arm. "You must be my grandfather," she said. "I was told the story by my mother of how you disappeared in the mountains."

Rip's granddaughter told him of how his wife had died and his daughter had moved away, but she invited him to live with her and her family. Rip soon settled in happily, and delighted in sitting his grandchildren on his knee and telling them of his adventure in the magical Catskill mountains.

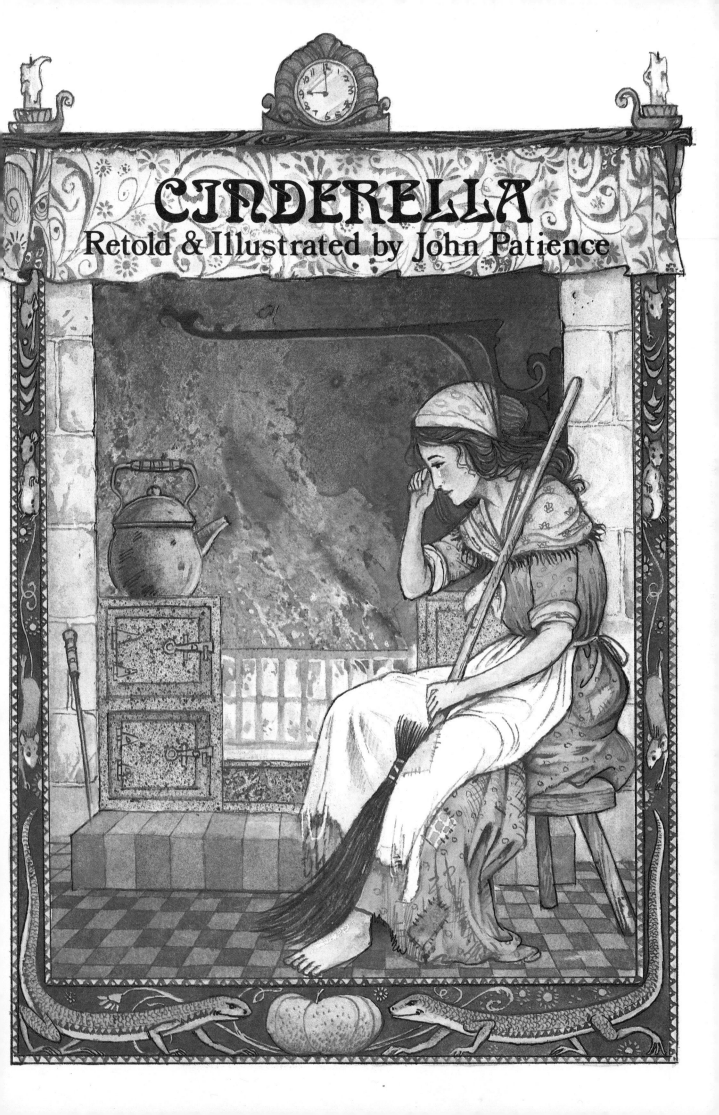

CINDERELLA
Retold & Illustrated by John Patience

"Cinderella, scrub the floor." "Cinderella, make the beds." "Cinderella, why is my dinner not ready yet?" This sort of thing was all that poor Cinderella heard from her step sisters from morning to night.

Cinderella was very beautiful and good natured but her step sisters, who were very ugly, were uncontrollably jealous of her so they made her life miserable.

One day a messenger called at the house with an invitation to a Grand Ball which the Prince was holding at the Palace. At once the step sisters were in a dither about what to wear and how they should look. "All the most handsome young men in the kingdom will be there," they cried. "We must be sure to look our best!" "Oh please can I come to the ball?" begged Cinderella. The ugly sisters howled with laughter. "You go to the ball . . . don't be so ridiculous. Just look how tattered your clothes are. You can't go looking like that, and besides, we will need you to help us get ready."

Anyone but Cinderella would have refused to help, but she was so kind hearted that she could not. On the night of the ball the ugly sisters had Cinderella running around in circles after them. "Powder my wig . . . Press my gown . . . Do this up . . . Fetch me a mirror and do hurry up you lazy creature." Cinderella felt quite dizzy by the time they were finished and she didn't even get so much as a "thank you." Her step sisters swept out to their carriage and left poor Cinderella crying quietly by the fireside.

Suddenly there was a flash of light and, to Cinderella's astonishment, a little old lady appeared. "I am your fairy godmother," she said. "Dry your eyes. You shall go to the ball. Just do as I say." First she sent Cinderella to the garden to find a pumpkin. She touched it with her magic wand and in an instant it became the most splendid coach you ever saw.

Then Cinderella was told to bring the mouse trap from the kitchen. Inside it were six white mice. The fairy godmother gave each of them a tap with her wand and turned them into snow white horses.

Next, Cinderella brought six little lizards which she found in a watering can.

These were turned into six footmen with silver-buttoned coats.

Finally a large black rat was transformed into a jolly coachman.

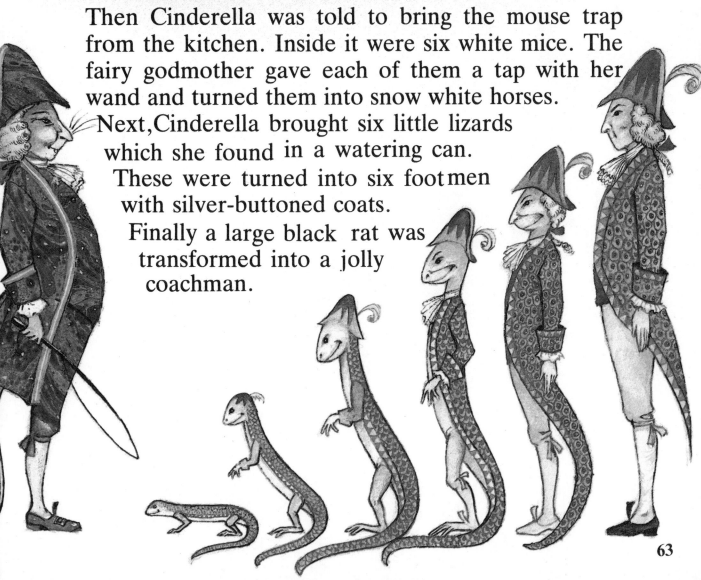

"Well now, child — you can go to the ball after
all," chuckled the fairy godmother. "Aren't you
pleased?" "Oh yes," exclaimed Cinderella, "But
how can I go in these old rags?" At once the
godmother waved her wand and the dirty old clothes
were changed into a beautiful ball gown and around
Cinderella's neck was a string of pearls. Then, to

complete the picture, she found a pair of dainty glass slippers on her feet. "Now, off you go and enjoy yourself," said the fairy godmother. "But remember, you must not stay a second after midnight or all your fine clothes will turn back into rags and the coach and horses, coachman and footmen will return to what they were before I worked my magic."

Cinderella arrived at the palace just as the ball was about to begin. As she entered the ballroom a murmur ran around the crowd. "Who is that beautiful girl?" The Prince could not take his eyes off her. He insisted that she dance with him for the entire evening. Cinderella had never been so happy before in her entire life. She was so happy that she didn't notice the time flying by until, suddenly, the

clock began to strike twelve. "Good heavens!" she cried, remembering her fairy godmother's warning. "I must go." She ran out into the darkness. At the twelfth stroke her fine clothes became rags and the coach turned back into a pumpkin. The Prince ran after Cinderella but she had vanished into the night. All that remained was one of her glass slippers. It had fallen from her foot as she ran down the palace steps. "I will find the girl who wore this slipper," vowed the Prince. "And I will make her my bride."

The next morning a proclamation was read out in the square to the sound of a trumpet. Every girl in the kingdom was to try on the glass slipper and whoever it fitted would marry the Prince. From North and South, East and West, people came flocking to the city. Young and old, short and tall, thin and fat, one by one they tried on the glass slipper, but it fitted none of them.

Eventually the slipper was brought to Cinderella's house. The ugly sisters were so excited. They snatched the glass slipper from the messenger before he could say a word. "Look! It fits me!" cried the elder sister. "Nonsense," said the younger sister. "Your heel is sticking out. Let me try it on. There it fits me like a glove." "Well, it certainly doesn't fit like a slipper!" sneered the elder one. "Your toes are bent double." "Does anyone else live here?" asked the messenger. "Everyone must try on the slipper." "Only Cinderella," replied the sisters. "But she's only a servant girl. The slipper can't possibly fit her." But the messenger insisted that even Cinderella must try on the slipper, and so she was brought from the kitchen where she had been cooking dinner. Slowly, she took the slipper and put it on. The ugly sisters gasped in amazement. "It fits," they wailed.

Then Cinderella's fairy godmother appeared and tapped her with the magic wand. Once more she was dressed in fine clothes, even more beautiful than her ball gown. "Your carriage is waiting to take you to the palace," said the fairy godmother. The Prince was overjoyed to see Cinderella again. Soon the couple were married. Everyone went to the wedding, even the ugly sisters whom Cinderella had completely forgiven for their previous unkindness.

Hansel & Gretel
Retold and Illustrated by John Patience

Once upon a time there were two children named Hansel and Gretel who lived with their parents on the edge of a great forest. Their father was a Woodcutter who worked very hard, but even so, the family was very poor.

One day, the Woodcutter's wife said to him, "Husband, we have no money left and there is not enough food in the larder to feed us all. There is only one thing to do. You must take the children deep into the forest and leave them there, or we shall all starve."

Unknown to their parents, Hansel and Gretel had overheard the conversation. "Don't worry," whispered Hansel to his sister, "I have thought of a plan to save us."

The next morning their mother gave Hansel and Gretel a crust of bread each and told them to save it for lunch. Then sadly she waved them goodbye.

The poor Woodcutter led his children into the forest. But as he walked, Hansel crumbled up his bread to leave a trail of breadcrumbs, so that he and his sister could find their way back home.

At last, deep in the forest, they stopped. The Wood-cutter told his children to gather some sticks and build a fire. When the fire was burning brightly, he said, "Now children, wait for me here. I am going off to chop wood. When I have finished I will come back for you." But the Woodcutter did not come back. As the children sat by the fire it grew darker and darker and the sounds of wild animals began to fill the forest.

Hansel and Gretel huddled together to comfort each other until, eventually, they both fell asleep. When they awoke the next morning, the children were eager to follow Hansel's trail of breadcrumbs back home, but the birds in the forest had seen Hansel laying the trail and had swooped down and eaten up all the crumbs.

"Never mind," said Gretel bravely. "Follow me. I shall soon have us home again." And so the two children set off through the forest. On and on they walked, but they were hopelessly lost and felt very hungry. They were beginning to think they might die of

hunger in the forest, when they came upon a snow white dove, singing on the branch of a tree.

The bird spread its wings and flew on a little way ahead of them. "It wants us to follow," cried Hansel.

They followed the dove until it arrived at a cottage and perched on the roof. It was the most extraordinary cottage they had ever seen! It was made of candy, cake, marzipan and barley sugar, and the windows were of clear spun sugar!

The children ran up to the house and the poor things were so hungry that they broke off pieces and ate them. Suddenly the door opened and a little old woman came out. "Ah, you poor children," she exclaimed. "You look very hungry." "We are," replied Gretel. "We are lost and have not had any food since yesterday."

So the old woman took the children inside and gave them all kinds of good things to eat and drink. The

cottage was as bright and clean as a new pin and the old lady had three fluffy white cats for pets. After they had eaten, the children were tired, so the old woman tucked them up in two little beds. "Sleep well," she said, "I will call you when it is time for breakfast."

But the old woman, who was really a wicked witch, came into the room in the night, and pulled Hansel out of bed. She locked him in a cage and said, "When you are fat I shall have you for my dinner!" The witch gave Hansel all the best and most fattening things to eat, but Gretel, who was made to do all the housework, was given only dry crusts to eat. The witch's house had been under a spell to make it look nice; now it appeared as it really was — dirty and untidy. As for the three fluffy white cats, they had turned into horrible, hissing, spiky, black things.

84

Every morning the old witch came to the cage and said, "Hansel, stretch out your finger so that I may feel whether you are getting fat." But Hansel used to stretch out a bone, and the old woman, who had very bad eyesight, thought it was his finger and wondered why he did not get fatter.

Finally, the witch decided she could not wait any longer for Hansel to get fat, and that she would eat him straight away, thin though he was. "I am going to bake some bread," said the crafty old woman to Gretel. "See if the oven is hot enough." Gretel replied, "I do not know how to do that. Our oven at home was different."

"You stupid child," cried the angry witch. "I'll show you. Watch me." And she opened the oven door. In an instant Gretel raced across the room and pushed the wicked witch inside and locked the door.

Then she let Hansel out of his cage. "Now we must search the house. I'm sure that the witch must have treasure hidden somewhere," said Hansel. And sure enough, the children found a great chest full of gold and precious stones. Gretel filled her apron with treasure and Hansel took a gold casket which he filled with jewels. Then they set off to find their way back home.

After walking for some time through the forest, the children came to a wide river. "I don't think we can get across," said Gretel. "We have no boat. What shall we do?" Close to the bank a large swan was gliding by. "Please help us," begged Hansel. The swan came to the bank. "Sit on my back," it said. "I will carry you safely across." The swan carried Hansel over the river and then went back for Gretel.

After thanking the swan, Hansel and Gretel went on a little way through a part of the forest which seemed to grow more and more familiar to them. At last, they saw their own house and at the door were their mother and father. The Woodcutter and his wife were overjoyed to see their children again, and welcomed them back with open arms. The treasure made them rich and they never went hungry again. And they all lived happily ever after.

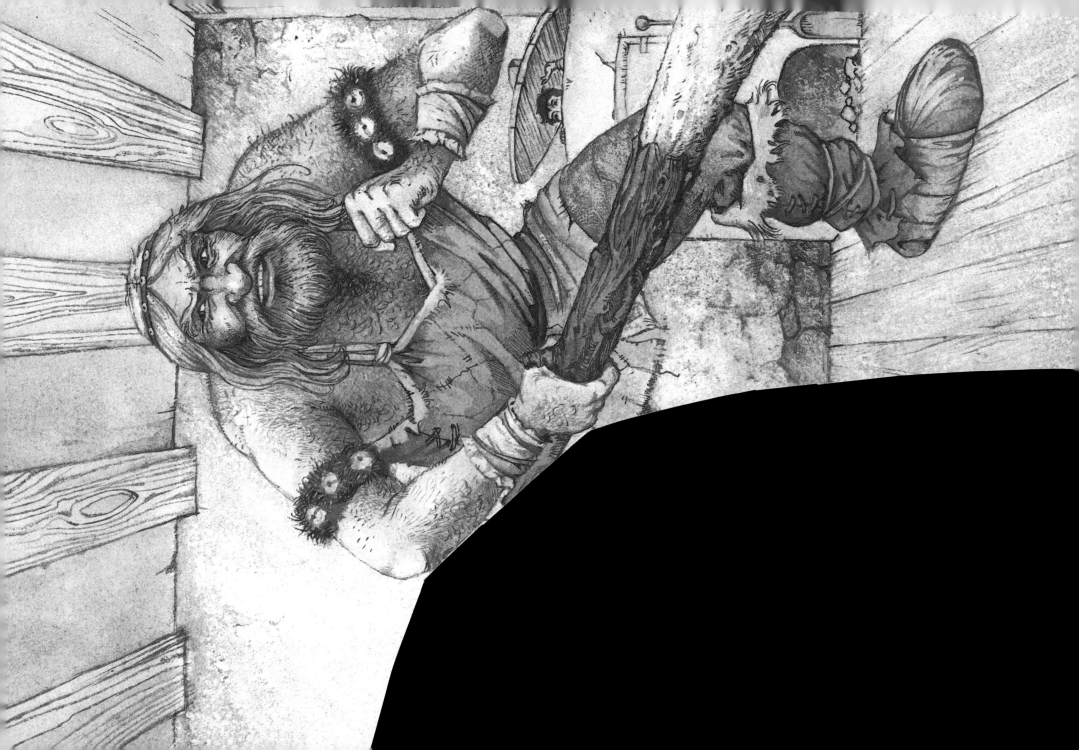

"Goodness! It's my husband," cried the giant's wife. "Quick, hide in the oven."

The giant's wife calmed her husband, telling him that he was mistaken. "It must be your porridge that you can smell," she said, putting a bowl on the table for him. The giant grunted and sat down. When he had finished eating he took some bags from a cupboard and poured out a shower of gold coins from one of them. He began to count them. "One, two, three. ." As he did this he grew sleepy and, by the time he had reached ten, he was fast asleep and snoring loudly. Jack had been watching the giant through a crack in the oven door. Now he leapt on to the table and, snatching a bag of gold coins, he made off with it.

Jack and his mother lived off the gold for a long
time, but at last it was all spent, and Jack decided
that he must climb the beanstalk again. The giant's
wife recognised Jack immediately and wanted to
know what had happened to the bag of gold. "I'll tell
you," said Jack, "if you give me breakfast." So the
giant's wife took him in and fed him. And again
there came the thudding of footsteps along the
passage and Jack was forced to hide himself. After
breakfast the giant's wife brought her husband a pet
hen. "Lay, little hen," commanded the giant and the
hen laid an egg of pure, glittering gold. After a while
the giant fell asleep. Then Jack crept out from his
hiding place, caught hold of the wonderful hen, ran
from the castle, slid down the beanstalk and was safe
and sound in his mother's garden.

101

Jack's mother was delighted with the hen which lay golden eggs. "We will never be poor again," she said. But before long Jack grew restless again and determined to climb the beanstalk. He realised that the giant's wife would not be pleased to see him, so he waited until she came out to hang out her washing, then crept into the castle and hid himself in a copper cauldron. Soon the giant came home and, sniffing the air, he bellowed,

"Fee, fie, foe, fum
I smell the blood of an Englishman."

But his wife assured him that he was mistaken. So he sat down to his breakfast, ate it and then called out. "Wife, bring me my harp." She brought it and placed it on the table. "Sing, harp," commanded the giant and the harp sang sweetly, lulling the giant off to sleep.

Then Jack crept quietly out of the cauldron and, tip-toeing over to the table, he snatched the harp and ran off with it. But this time he got a surprise, for the harp called out loudly, "Master, master!" and the giant woke up. Fear made Jack run like the wind, but the giant came lumbering after him, roaring for his blood. Jack leapt onto the beanstalk and started to climb down. The beanstalk began to shake and

THE PIED PIPER
of Hamelin

Retold & Illustrated by
John Patience

Long ago, the pretty little town of Hamelin in Germany suffered from a terrible plague of vermin. The town was overrun by huge rats. They scuttled over the tiled roof tops, infested cellars and found their way into every larder in the town. They ate their way through barrels of apples, devoured cheeses by the dozen and gobbled up the grain which the towns-folk had stored up for the Winter.

The rats were bold as brass and feared no one. They stole the food from tables, fought with the dogs and cats and bit the babies in their cradles. Naturally, the people of Hamelin did everything they could to get rid of the pests. They smoked them out of their holes and put poison down for them. But it was all to no avail. Every day that passed, the rats increased in number, growing fatter as the people grew thinner. All day and all night Hamelin was filled with the deafening noise of the rats squealing and gnawing, so that there was not forty winks of sleep to be had in the whole town.

At last, the townsfolk could stand it no longer. They marched in a great crowd to the Town Hall and demanded angrily that the Mayor and his Council should do something about the vermin. But what could they do?

The Mayor and the Councillors were afraid of the angry mob and of losing their jobs. They loved their beautiful fur-lined cloaks, their gold chains and the feeling of importance which these things gave them. "Surely someone can think of a way of ridding us of the rats," cried the Mayor. "We will offer a reward to the man who can come up with the answer." The Councillors agreed that this was a good idea.

So, the very next day a town crier was sent out to read a proclamation in the town square. He rang his bell and shouted loudly:

"THERE WILL BE A REWARD OF ONE THOUSAND GILDERS FOR WHOEVER IS ABLE TO RID HAMELIN OF ITS PLAGUE OF RATS."

Well, as you know, everyone was already trying to get rid of the rats, but now they tried even harder. Rat catchers came from all over Germany to try their luck. Huge traps were dug out and baited with giant cheeses, clever chemists concocted bubbling poisons to pour down the rat holes, but still the rats infested the town!

The people of Hamelin soon began to complain again. "What use are a Mayor and Councillors in fine robes if

112

they cannot rid us of the rats?" they wailed. Once more they marched to the Town Hall and beat upon the door. Inside the Mayor and his Council shook with fear.

Suddenly a great gust of wind blew through the hall, swirling around the marble pillars, and in the middle of it appeared a tall, thin stranger.

He was dressed in a most peculiar fashion, half in red and half in yellow. In his cap he wore a peacock feather. A mysterious smile played upon his lips, his eyes twinkled with a strange light and in his hand he carried a long, thin pipe.

"Who are you?" exclaimed the startled Mayor. "People call me the Pied Piper," answered the stranger. "I have come from halfway round the world to solve your problem and claim the reward. By means of my magic pipe I can rid Hamelin of its rats – no creature upon the earth can resist my music." The Mayor welcomed him warmly and begged him to begin his work at once, promising him not one thousand gilders but one hundred thousand if he succeeded.

The Pied Piper stepped out into the streets and began to play his music, dancing off lightly over the cobblestones. Then the rats began to appear, pouring like a squealing tide out of the houses; large rats, small rats, young rats, old rats, following the Piper as though their lives depended on it.

On and on the Piper danced all the way across the town, with the rats surging behind him, until at last he reached the River Weser. There he stepped into a boat and, continuing to play, he floated out over the deep, dark waters. After him came the rats. Pushing blindly to the river's edge, they threw themselves in. All through the night the Piper's music could be heard, accompanied by the terrible sounds of splashing and squealing, until by sunrise every last rat in Hamelin had been drowned.

That morning there was a great celebration in the town. But when the Pied Piper appeared in the Town Hall to claim his reward, no one appeared at all glad to see him. "One thousand gilders," laughed the Mayor, "that was merely a joke. Come take fifty." "One thousand gilders you promised," shouted the Pied Piper angrily, "and if you do not pay me you will soon wish you had. I can pipe other tunes as you will find out." "Go blow on your pipe until you burst," sneered the Mayor.

"Very well," said the Piper with a sinister smile. Then once again he stepped into the street and blew upon his magic pipe. This time the air was filled with a very different sort of music. It was strange and enchanting, better than the best fairy tale ever told. It was music which no child could resist. They came out from their houses laughing and chattering, not knowing where the Piper and his music would lead them, but happy and eager to follow.

The townspeople could only stand and watch, frozen
like statues by the enchantment of the music. Soon
every child in Hamelin was following the Piper and it
looked as if he was leading them down to the River
Weser. "Are we to see our children drowned?" thought
the horrified parents. But no, as they watched the Piper
turned west towards Koppelberg Hill. Then a great sigh
of relief went up from Hamelin. "He can't possibly lead
our children over Koppelberg," thought the people.
"The hill is far too steep. He will surely have to stop."

But, unbelievably, as he advanced the side of the hill
opened up before him and the Piper, followed by the
children, disappeared inside. Then the hill closed up
again, crashing together with a sound like thunder.

Only one child was left behind – a little lame boy who
had not been able to keep up with the rest. He returned
home sad and disappointed, knowing that he would
never see the enchanted land the music had promised to
lead him to.

Without the children, Hamelin was a quiet, unhappy place for many years afterwards. The Mayor and his Council were chased out of the town and a warning was carved on a stone by Koppelberg Hill that a promise once made should always be kept, especially if it is made to a piper dressed in red and yellow.

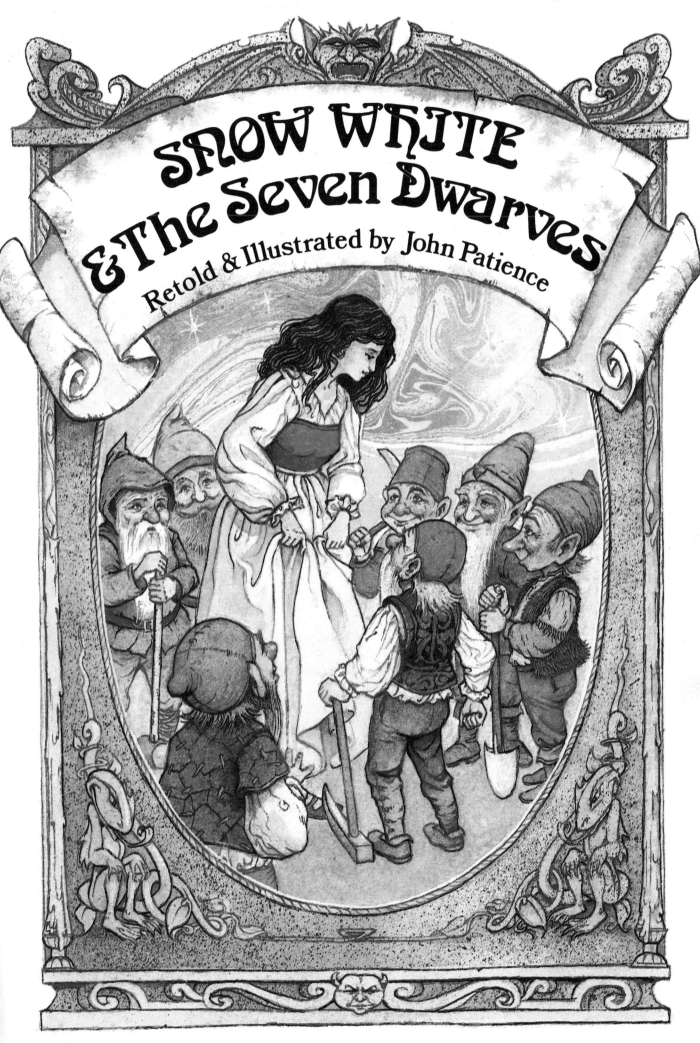

SNOW WHITE
& The Seven Dwarves
Retold & Illustrated by John Patience

Once upon a time a queen sat sewing by her window. Snow flakes were falling outside, and as she watched them settling on her black ebony windowsill, she pricked her finger with the needle and a drop of red blood fell onto the snow. Then she thought to herself, "I wish I had a daughter with skin as white as that snow, with cheeks as red as blood and hair as ebony black as the window frame."

Strangely, the queen's wish came true and she gave birth to a beautiful baby girl whom she named Snow White. But alas the queen died when Snow White was born and before long the king married again.

The new queen was very beautiful but she was evil and vain and could not bear to think that anyone might be lovelier than she. She had a magic mirror which she would look into every day, saying:

"Mirror, mirror on the wall,
Who is the fairest of them all?"
The mirror's answer was always the same:
"Thou art the fairest,"
until one fateful day, when Snow White had grown up, it replied:
"Thou art fair and beauteous to see,
But Snow White is fairer far than thee."
At these words the queen flew into a terrible rage. She called a servant and ordered him to take Snow White into the forest and kill her!

The servant knew he was meant to kill Snow White, but he couldn't do it, so he left her in the forest at the mercy of the weather and the wild beasts.

Soon Snow White began to feel frightened and hungry. She wandered around, looking for berries that she might eat. Suddenly she saw a tiny cottage. She went up to the door and knocked. There was no answer so she went inside. The room was cosy and warm and the table was laid for supper. A stew bubbled in the pot which hung over the fire. The smell was irresistible and Snow White helped herself to some. Then, feeling sleepy, she went upstairs and lay down on one of the seven little beds she found there.

Presently in came the owners of the cottage – seven little dwarfs who worked in the mountains digging for gold. They saw immediately that all was not right; there was a dirty plate on the table! They all crept up the stairs and then one of them whispered, "Look, someone is sleeping in my bed!" His brothers were filled with wonder and astonishment and came with their lamps to look at

Snow White. "Good heavens! What a lovely child she is," they whispered. The dwarfs were delighted to find her and took great care not to wake her, but fussed around as quietly as little mice, tucking her in and making her snug.

The next morning, Snow White told the dwarfs her story and they took pity on her. They decided to let her live in their cottage with them, and in return she could keep the place clean and cook their meals while they were out digging for gold. Snow White soon settled into her new home and was very happy because the dwarfs were much kinder to her than her stepmother had been.

It seemed that Snow White would live happily
ever after with the seven dwarfs, until one day her
stepmother looked into the magic mirror and asked
it who was the fairest in the land.

"Queen, thou art of beauty rare,"
replied the mirror,

"But Snow White living in the glen,
With the seven little men,
Is a thousand times more fair."

When the queen realised that her servant had
deceived her and Snow White was still alive, she
was terribly angry. She locked herself in a secret
room in the castle and brewed a horrible poison
which she put into a beautiful, rosy, red apple.
Then, disguised as a gipsy, the queen set out for the
dwarfs' cottage.

The evil queen knocked on the cottage door and begged to be let in, but the dwarfs had warned Snow White not to open the door to strangers and so she refused. "Silly girl," said the queen, "I've brought you a lovely apple. Take it."

"Oh, what harm can it do?" thought Snow White. She opened the door and took a bite from the apple. Immediately she fell down dead upon the floor.

When the dwarfs found Snow White they were all heartbroken. They tried every way they could to revive her, but it was no good. At last they gave up hope and made her a beautiful crystal coffin, which they placed in a forest glade. Every day they brought fresh flowers and placed them around the coffin and wept for her.

One day a Prince came riding by. When he saw Snow White he fell in love with her and, opening her coffin, he lifted her in his arms. As he did so the piece of apple which the dwarfs didn't realise was lodged in her throat, fell from her mouth. She opened her eyes and fell in love with the prince at first sight.

The wicked queen could not believe it when her mirror said,

"Oh queen, although you are of beauty rare,

The Prince's bride is a thousand times more fair."
She was so furious that she choked and died.

Now Snow White had nothing to fear from the wicked queen and she lived happily ever after with her prince in a fine palace, where they were often visited by seven dwarfs.

GOLDILOCKS
and
The Three Bears

Retold & Illustrated by John Patience

Once upon a time there was a little girl called Goldilocks who lived on the edge of a great forest. She was called Goldilocks because she had very beautiful curly blond hair which gleamed like gold in the sunlight. But although Goldilocks looked so pretty she could sometimes be very naughty. Every day as Goldilocks went out to play, her mother would remind her: ''Now Goldilocks, you may go and play in the meadow, but don't go into the wood, or you will get lost.''

One morning Goldilocks began to grow tired of playing on the swing in the meadow. She couldn't catch any minnows in the stream and even her favourite doll seemed boring. ''I know,'' said Goldilocks to herself, ''I'll go exploring in the forest!'' She glanced back at the house to make sure her mother wasn't watching, then off she ran across the meadow and into the forest.

Goldilocks wandered deeper and deeper into the forest until, at last, she became completely lost. The trees began to appear menacing, she imagined she could see faces in them, peering down at her; and once she thought she heard a deep growling noise like the sound of a wild animal. She felt very frightened and was about to cry when, to her surprise, she saw a strange little cottage amongst the trees. It was thatched with fur! Goldilocks tapped on the door but there was no answer. Then she peeped in through an open window. There was no one home so Goldilocks climbed inside for a look around.

Inside the cottage a log fire was burning brightly and a table was laid for breakfast with three bowls of steaming porridge. It smelled delicious and Goldilocks suddenly realised how hungry she was. "I'll just try a little to see how it tastes," she said. First she tried the largest bowl, but it was too salty. Next she tried the middle-sized bowl, but it was too sweet. Finally she tried the little bowl. "That's just right," she cried and she ate it all up.

Round the fireside were three chairs. Feeling tired, Goldilocks decided to sit down. First she tried the big chair, but it was very uncomfortable. Next she tried the middle-sized chair, but that was no better. Then she tried the little chair, but it was too small and broke into pieces.

In the corner of the room was a staircase and Goldilocks climbed up to see what was at the top. There she found a bedroom with three beds in it – and of course, one was very big, one was middle-sized and one was small. She tried each bed in turn. The large one was too hard, the middle-sized one was too soft, but the little one was just right, and Goldilocks soon fell fast asleep.

Goldilocks would not have slept so peacefully if she had known that the cottage belonged to three bears, and at that moment they were coming down the woodland path on their way home. Father bear and baby bear had been collecting firewood, and mother bear had collected a basket full of blackberries. "I do hope the porridge you made for breakfast will be cool enough to eat now," said baby bear to his mother as the cottage came into view. "I am very hungry."

As soon as they got into the house, the three bears went to the table to eat up their porridge. "Somebody," growled father bear in his big gruff voice, "Somebody has been eating my porridge." "Somebody," said mother bear in her medium-sized voice, "Somebody has been eating my porridge too." "And somebody has been eating my porridge, and eaten it all up!" cried baby bear in his baby-sized voice.

Then father bear noticed that the pipe he had left on his chair had been brushed off onto the floor. "Who's been sitting in my chair?" he roared in his great big voice.

"Who's been sitting in my chair?" said mother bear in her medium-sized voice. "And who's been sitting in my chair and broken it all to pieces?" cried poor little baby bear in his tiny little voice.

"Look, someone has left muddy footprints," growled father bear. "They go all the way up the stairs."

As soon as they were inside the bedroom, father bear growled in his big gruff voice, "Somebody has been lying on my bed." "Somebody has been lying on my bed too," said mother bear in her medium-sized voice. "Somebody has been lying on my bed," cried baby bear, "and they're still there, fast asleep!"

The three bears gathered around and stared in astonishment at the pretty little girl with golden curls. Who on earth was she? And what was she doing in their cottage?

Goldilocks woke up with a start and rubbed her eyes. She thought that the three bears were part of her dream, so she pinched herself hard, but the bears did not disappear. Now she was very frightened. "Goodness me, you're real!" she cried and, jumping out of bed, she ran down the stairs and out through the front door. On and on she ran, not stopping for breath until at last she reached the edge of the forest and saw her own house, with her mother waiting on the doorstep for her. And she never went exploring in the forest again!